The Hottest Boy Who Ever Lived

Anna Fienberg
Illustrated by Kim Gamble

A LITTLE ARK BOOK

ALLEN & UNWIN

Hector lived beside a volcano at the very edge of the world.
He had flaming red hair and a pet salamander,
and he slept in a treehouse in the jungle.

He ate mangoes for breakfast and pineapples for lunch,
and nobody told him when to go to bed.

But Hector was sad. He was unbearably, bone-achingly sad.

'No offence, Minton,' he said to his salamander, 'but I would give up
my mangoes, my treehouse, even my view of the volcano,
just for someone to talk to.'

'**W**hat about me? You can tell *me* anything,' said Minton.

'Yes, but one salamander is just not enough.'

Minton was a loyal pet, and in his heart he agreed. 'It is a terrible shame, Hector, especially when you have such a great talent for conversation. But who else could ever be your friend? I mean, with *your* problem.'

For Hector, you see, was the hottest boy who ever lived.

Inside, he burned like a bonfire.

When he sighed, the grass turned brown.

Hector sighed now, and the grass smoked.

Living on the edge of the world, as he did, Hector had never known a family, or friends. Minton, who could dance through fire, was the only creature that could bear to be near him.

'The first time I saw you,' Minton told him, 'you were shooting right out of the volcano.'

Hector couldn't remember back that far, but he had always known Minton.

'I'd give anything for a hug,' Hector whispered to Minton one day.
'I'd settle for a cuddle from an octopus, a squeeze from a boa constrictor,
even a lick from a lion.'

Minton looked at him sadly. He could hardly fit around Hector's big toe.

'I know,' said Minton, 'but even the mosquitoes won't come near you.
Believe me, I've been around, and this is the best place for you. Really,
Hector, you are just too hot to handle.'

That night a terrible storm swept over the jungle. Lightning knifed the sky, and trees crashed down. Clouds burst like balloons, flooding the jungle. Hector found himself on the ground, clinging to his fallen tree, and all around him the water was rising!

The tree began to roll, and was swept out to sea.

Hector clung on. Soon he could no longer see the beach, or his jungle, or even the volcano. Ahead stretched the dark grey ocean.

Hector shivered. Now he was truly alone in the world.

'Oh, Minton,' he cried, 'where are you?'

Minton crawled out from a hole in the tree.

'We are in deep trouble,' he said, 'but at least we're together.'

Hector and Minton watched the sun come up and go down many times while they floated on the endless sea. Minton's skin dried out like leather, and Hector was starving.

But then Hector noticed something new.

'Wind!' he said. 'Do you feel it, Minton?'

'Yes, it's making me shiver. I've never felt anything as cold as this.'

'But I thought you'd been around.'

'Well,' said Minton, 'there's "around" and "*around*". For a small salamander like me, getting to the volcano and back was something.'

Then Hector noticed another thing. Out of the mist loomed enormous blocks of whiteness.

'Land!' cried Hector. But when he drew near, the blocks began to dribble and melt, until they finally disappeared.

'A mirage,' said Minton darkly. 'A trick of the eyes. Prepare yourself, Hector. This is the end, and these are the day-dreams of death!'

But now, coming towards them, was another day-dream. It wasn't white, and it wasn't melting. It was a small wooden boat, paddled by a girl with golden hair.

'Ahoy there!' the vision cried. And when she pulled up close to Hector's tree she put out her hand to shake.

'I'm Gilda the Adventurer,' she said.

Her hair was like woven sunlight.

Shyly, Hector put his hand into hers.

'I'm Hector,' he said, 'and you'd better watch out, because I'm rather hot.'

Hector held his breath and hung on to her hand. He tingled with joy and comfort and delight.

'Thundering Thor, you're as hot as fire!' gasped Gilda, but she gripped his hand even harder. She was warm for the first time in her life.

'Mmm,' she said, 'I could hold on to you for ever!'

Hector closed his eyes with happiness.

Perhaps living on the hot edge of the world had not been the best place for him.

Where Gilda lived the winds were freezing, and snow was thick on the ground.
The people wore heavy cloaks and boots, even at home. They were Vikings,
with blue eyes and blond hair, and they had never seen a boy like Hector.

'Look at his flaming red hair!' they cried. 'Don't touch him, he burns
like fire!' They trembled with fear at the sight of him.

None of the Vikings would talk to Hector. When he came near they hurried
away, calling out, 'Demon! Dragon! Take your evil magic away from here!'

And they didn't much like Minton, either.

'I hate to be a told-you-so,' said Minton, 'but I told you so. The volcano is the best place for you.'

'Yes,' said Hector. 'I'm lonelier here, amongst all these people, than I ever was in my treehouse. The truth is, I *am* too hot to handle.'

But Gilda was not called an Adventurer for nothing. She was not afraid. She had seen much of the world in her small wooden boat, and she was hungry to know more.

Gilda took Hector and Minton into her house at night. To keep the silence away, Hector would tell her marvellous tales. He told her about the volcano, and its belly of fire, about the lava that glowed red in the night, and about the mangoes that were as soft as velvet.

But the Vikings were still afraid. Every day their anger grew. When the fishing was bad, they blamed Hector. When the chickens didn't lay, they blamed Hector. It was the coldest winter anyone could remember, and they all agreed it was Hector, the stranger, who had brought bad luck.

'Something terrible will happen soon,' Minton told Hector. And it did.

One morning, at dawn, Minton woke to see a crowd of people passing the house. They were wailing into the bitter air, and Minton saw a child lying stiff and frozen in her mother's arms.

'She fell into the ice,' the Vikings whispered to each other. 'It was that demon, Hector, who caused it!'

'Wake up, Hector!' urged Minton. 'Something terrible has happened. And they're saying it's your fault!'

Hector peeped outside.

The crowd parted fearfully as he walked up to the child.
He looked at her blue lips and her face as pale as marble.

Gently he took her into his arms and breathed on her cheeks, her hands, her eyelids.

The crowd was silent. Only the cracking wind whipped across the ice.

And then the child opened her eyes.

Her cheeks shone pink. She smiled at Hector.

'How warm you are,' she murmured, and snuggled closer.

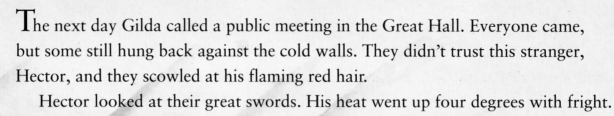

The next day Gilda called a public meeting in the Great Hall. Everyone came, but some still hung back against the cold walls. They didn't trust this stranger, Hector, and they scowled at his flaming red hair.

Hector looked at their great swords. His heat went up four degrees with fright.

Gilda came forward and said, 'Yesterday some of you saw Hector save little Asa from the ice. Now see what else he can do!'

In the centre of the hall sat twelve huge barrels of water. Hector dipped his hand into them, one after the other, and soon water bubbled and popped. The air warmed, and people began taking off their cloaks.

'You see? Hot baths for everyone!' cried Gilda.

Hector blew on some stones until they glowed red. When Gilda tossed water over them the stones hissed, and steam rose in hot spirals. People smiled and took off their leggings.

'Enjoy the sauna!' Gilda invited them.

Hector held out his hands, and Gilda put barley cakes on his palms to toast. Children lined up to take a piece.

'Anyone for honey?' Gilda said.

All around the hall, Viking faces were relaxing with the warmth, and the children smiled shyly at Hector.

Hector smiled back.

He found that if he concentrated he could become even hotter. He fried eggs on his shoulders, and barbecued salmon fillets on his feet.

Now everyone was lining up to stand near Hector. Some had hurried home and returned with chestnuts to roast in his hands. Others wanted their frozen chickens thawed. And some just wanted to be hugged till their toes tingled.

Soon Vikings were asking Hector home to boil their water and clear snow from their doors. He melted holes in the ice for fishing, and heated the animals' barns. Minton always kept him company, and when they stayed for dinner Minton was served a special plate of roasted worms with beetle sauce.

Gilda was so pleased with Hector and the Vikings that she decided to stop adventuring and start a business: *Hector's Heating and Hot Water Service*. She bought a sled and a pony, and together they toured the freezing villages, bringing warmth and happiness.

Hector loved his new life. He loved the hugging and the smiles and the great conversation. He loved being famous.
But best of all he loved the cold winter nights when Gilda and Minton curled around his heat, swapping stories and making plans for the great adventures to come.